Translation copyright © 1984 by Viking Penguin Inc./All rights reserved/Originally
published in 1983 as *Titta, Madicken, Det Snöar* by Rabén & Sjögren Bokforlag,
Stockholm./Copyright © 1983: text: Astrid Lindgren; Illustrations: Ilon Wikland
Published in 1984 by The Viking Press, 40 West 23rd Street, New York, N.Y. 10010
Published simultaneously in Canada by Penguin Books Canada Limited
Printed in Italy
2 3 4 5 88 87 86 85
Library of Congress Cataloging in Publication Data/Lindgren, Astrid, 1907–   The
runaway sleigh ride./Translation of: Titta, Madicken, det snöar!/Summary: On a
snowy day in a small Swedish village, mischievous Elizabeth gets into trouble when
she hides on the back of a farmer's sleigh and is taken for a very long ride.
[1. Snow—Fiction.   2. Sleds—Fiction.   3. Sweden—Fiction]
I. Wikland, Ilon, ill.   II. Title.
PZ7.L6585It   1984   [E]   83-23347   ISBN 0-670-40454-3

ASTRID LINDGREN

The Runaway
Sleigh Ride

Illustrated by Ilon Wikland

The Viking Press
New York

Today all of Primrose Hill is sleeping late because it is Sunday and a dark winter's morning. But soon they all wake up, one after another. Gossie the cat and Sasso the dog in the kitchen, Alva in the back room, Mummy and Daddy in their bedroom, and Elizabeth in her room, which is Mardie's room too. But Mardie is still asleep and doesn't want to wake up.

Elizabeth knows how to bring her big sister to life. She lets up the blind with a *thwack* and the next instant cries out:

"Look, Mardie, it's snowing!"

At this Mardie leaps out of bed. The first snow—there really is something weird and wonderful about it.

"I like this snow more than any other," says Mardie.

"Well, I like every bit of snow in the whole wide world," Elizabeth declares.

That makes Mardie laugh.

"What can you do with all the snow in the whole world? I think we've got enough snow of our own."

And now the snow is falling thick and fast all over Primrose Hill.

Elizabeth and Mardie romp in the snow all day. They roll themselves in it, they make a snowman, and then they roll themselves in the snow again. So does Sasso. Through the kitchen window peers Gossie, thinking that Sasso has gone mad. Gossie does not understand about snow.

But Daddy does. All at once, out he dashes to join in.

"Now I'll show you how I can knock the snowman's nose off with this snowball," he says.

And he does.

"Well, now I'll show you how I can knock *your* nose off with this snowball," says Mardie.

And then there is a snowball fight. Daddy ends up falling into a snowdrift. He roars with laughter but does not want to continue the fight. At the kitchen window Mummy stands and looks on, thinking that Daddy has gone mad. She does not understand about snow any more than Gossie does!

The following day Mardie has a fever and has to stay in bed. What bad luck, because today she was going to buy Christmas presents with Alva and Elizabeth, and afterward she was going to bake gingerbread with Mummy.

"But I know someone who hasn't got a fever," says Elizabeth.

"And I can be with Alva by myself now."

That makes Mardie angry.

"Wicked child," she says.

Elizabeth thinks that is unfair.

"Well, it's you I'm going to buy a present for, you know! But perhaps I won't now if you're going to be so stupid."

Alva has to come over and cheer Mardie up.

"You and I'll go and buy Christmas presents another day. All by ourselves!"

Mummy comes over to cheer her up, too.

"Perhaps you can bake some gingerbread anyway. But you can't go walking around the town getting freezing cold."

"You have to look after yourself," says Elizabeth, coming over and trying to tuck Mardie in with great vigor. But Mardie does not want to be tucked in. Not by someone who hasn't got a temperature and is going to buy Christmas presents!

It is a marvelous day in town. All the shop windows look so wonderful! Alva and Elizabeth walk around taking a good look at everything.

It's nice being with Alva, thinks Elizabeth. She never says: "Come on now, we have to hurry!"

"Come on now, we have to hurry," says Alva just then. "To the toy shop!" But Elizabeth wants to hurry to the toy shop, because that is where she is going to buy a Christmas present for Mardie.

And that takes time. Elizabeth would like to buy almost everything on the shelves. Though maybe not all for her sister.

Elizabeth points to a toy doll in a sailor's outfit. "Ooh, he's so sweet he gives me the shivers!" declares Elizabeth.

"Well, you'd better pick something for Mardie now so she gets the shivers on Christmas Eve," says Alva.

And so Elizabeth buys a puzzle for Mardie. On the box there is a picture of a kitten that has tipped over a saucer of milk.

Alva puts the package in her bag.

"Mardie will be pleased with this, I reckon!"

"Yes, otherwise I can have it myself," says Elizabeth.

Alva laughs at this.

"Oh, no. Anyway, you'll have to wait outside for a minute now because I want to buy a few things too."

"What sort of things?" says Elizabeth.

"It's a secret," says Alva. "Outside with you now! And don't go walking off anywhere, promise!"

Elizabeth promises. She waits outside patiently and tries to peek through the window to see if Alva is standing anywhere near that boy doll.

There are a lot of horses and sleighs in town today. Old farmers come to sell their Christmas trees and birchwood and potatoes and apples. All of a sudden a sleigh appears from the direction of the square, and Elizabeth's eyes nearly pop out of her head when she sees Mr. Svenson's little boy, Gustav, sneaking a ride on the back runners! Elizabeth knows him; he lives not far from Primrose Hill.

"Bet *you* don't dare do this," he calls out to Elizabeth as he passes by. But Elizabeth calls back: "Yes, I do dare."

"No, you don't, you're just a little girl," cries Gustav. And Elizabeth snorts because she is bigger than little Gustav anyway!

But the sleigh has already carried Gustav off into the distance. Then a new sleigh appears and stops right outside the toy shop. The man driving gets off to deliver a sack of wood to an old lady in the house opposite. She sticks her head out of the window and shouts: "Here you are at last, Andersson!"

While Andersson is off delivering the sack of wood, Elizabeth stands on the back runners to see what it feels like. It doesn't seem dangerous at all. Gustav needn't have been so cocky about it! But what is Alva doing all this time? Is she buying the whole toy shop?

Then Andersson comes back. He pats his mare.

"Now it's off home to Fallebo, old girl!"

And off he goes. But just as the sleigh starts off, Elizabeth hops onto the runners and stands there, just like Gustav! Though Andersson doesn't know she's there.

He *is* going a bit fast, thinks Elizabeth. But I'll jump off the next time he stops.

The sleigh really moves along. Elizabeth swishes through the town to the accompaniment of sleigh bells, and it feels marvelous. What a shame little Gustav can't see her now!

But it would be nice if Andersson decided to stop soon. Before Alva has finished her shopping.

But Andersson doesn't stop. He's in a hurry to get home to Fallebo, and it is a long way to go.

"C'mon now, girl, get along there," he says, brandishing the whip. And the mare moves quickly because she wants to get home too. Elizabeth has also started to wish she were at home. She would like to shout to Andersson to make him stop, but she doesn't dare, and he drives on and on. Soon they are far from the town and Elizabeth is afraid. They pass several farms and each time she hopes that it will be Fallebo.

But it isn't. Soon they are in the forest. Nothing but snowy fir trees to be seen. Elizabeth is so sorry she jumped on to this awful sleigh that won't ever stop! Not even when Andersson drinks from the bottle he has with him. He can drive with the reins in one hand and the bottle in the other. And he sings too.

Here's to making merry!
Here's to getting drunk!

He sings other things too that are even worse.

But Elizabeth cannot hold out any longer.

"Stop," she yells, "I want to get off!"

Andersson turns his head and sees her. And now, at last, the sleigh comes to a halt. But Andersson is angry.

"Have you been there all the way from town?"

"Ye-es," weeps Elizabeth. "And now I want to go home!"

"Well, you'd better get a move on, then," says Andersson.

Elizabeth weeps even harder.

"Yes, but you'll have to take me!"

"That's what you think! Nobody asked you to jump on my sleigh. There's the road! Start walking!"

And Andersson drives off, leaving Elizabeth standing there. She hears him strike up his horrid song again. But soon nothing is to be heard. No singing and no tinkling of sleigh bells! Just the faint whispering of the wind in the trees!

Now I'll die, thinks Elizabeth. Alone on a snowy road in the middle of the forest so far from home. She starts to run. She runs and runs for all she is worth. It is not so easy running and crying at the same time. In the end, she has to stop. And she stands there in the snow, weeping and calling:

"Mummy! Mummy, I want you!"

But Mummy can't hear. She is just about to start baking gingerbread, at home on Primrose Hill.

"I don't understand why they're taking so long," she says to Mardie. "We can't wait any longer, we'll have to start baking!"

Yes, it looks like they're going to buy up the whole town before they come home, thinks Mardie. She doesn't feel sick any more, and now there is going to be some baking done around here. Mummy has made up two large lumps of gingerbread dough, one for Mardie and one for Elizabeth. Mardie starts baking gingerbread animals in long rows. But without Elizabeth, it is not as much fun, and she longs for Elizabeth to come rushing through the

door, crying: "Have you started already?"

But only Alva comes. Alone! Poor Alva has looked everywhere for Elizabeth!

"Has Elizabeth come home?" she asks anxiously. And when she finds out that Elizabeth has not, Alva cries so hard the tears gush out.

"But she promised she wouldn't go walking off anywhere!"

Mummy turns pale when she hears the full story.

"Where on earth can the child have gone?"

And she telephones Daddy at work.

"What shall we do? You'll have to go into town and look!"

"I already have," says Alva, as she sits among the baking pans, crying.

Meanwhile, Elizabeth is struggling homeward through the snowdrifts. But the road never ends! And why, for heaven's sake, must it be snowing so hard? Yet it was she who said she liked every bit of snow.

"Not this wretched snow, anyway! And not any other snow either, so there!"

She is angry, which makes it easier to make her way through the snow. But soon she is just miserable again. Miserable and tired and hungry, and all alone. How can everything be so horrible?

"Mummy," she cries. "Mummy, I want you!"

Then all of a sudden she sees a cottage a little way off the road. Surely there must be some kind person there who can help her? She wastes no time and, sobbing, plods through the snow to the cottage and bangs on the door. But no one opens up, there's no one at home. Then she sobs so hard her whole body trembles. Poor Elizabeth. If Mummy could hear her now, she would surely cry too.

But next to the cottage is a little cow shed. Perhaps there are people there? Elizabeth bangs on the shed door. There comes such a bellow from the inside that she jumps in the air. Maybe they only keep angry bulls in this cow shed. But she wants to get in there, where it is a little warm at least. She tries the door. What luck! It isn't locked.

Inside a cow stands there alone in its stall. And she bellows even more when Elizabeth walks in. But soon she quiets down and looks at Elizabeth with kindly cow eyes.

Elizabeth pats her cautiously. Just a cow! Well then, she is not quite so all alone in the world!

It is nice in this cow shed, and Elizabeth feels a *little* relieved. There is some straw in an empty stall, so she lies down there to sleep for a while. But soon she wakes up shivering. She pats the cow and warms herself a little against her. But then she goes out into the snow again.

"I have to get home before I simply die!
Stupid old Andersson!"

And trudging through the snow, struggling and crying, Elizabeth makes her way
a bit at a time. But finally she is so tired
that she falls by the roadside, and that is
the last straw:

"That's it! I'm not getting up any
more!"

But it is dangerous to lie out in the
snow, she has heard. Unless you dig yourself in so that you don't freeze to death!
She tosses a little snow on to her stomach,
but it doesn't help much.

But the way it's snowing now, I'll soon
be as good as buried anyway, she thinks.

Then suddenly she hears singing and
the tinkling of bells approaching. What, is
it old Andersson coming back?

No, it is not Andersson. It is Mr. and
Mrs. Hansson from Kullebo, driving along.
Elizabeth darts out and shouts with all her
might:

"Can you give me a ride?"

"Dear child," says Mrs. Hansson when
she sees Elizabeth standing like a little
snowman by the roadside. "What
are you doing out here alone
in the forest?"

Elizabeth bursts into tears and cannot answer. And Mr. Hansson brushes the snow off her and lifts her up to sit her in his wife's lap.

"There, there, it's all right now," says Mrs. Hansson. And Mrs. Hansson wraps her warm shawl around her and tucks her feet in under the sheepskin rug they have over their knees and takes off her wet mittens and warms her hands in her own and holds her tight in her arms. It really is nice, it really is wonderful, but Elizabeth cries all the same. Finally, she stops sobbing, though, and tells them what her name is and where she lives and why she is so far from home.

"Oh, you poor little thing," says Mrs. Hansson over and over. And Mr. Hansson urges on his horse.

"Don't cry now! We're taking you home to Mummy!"

And Mr. and Mrs. Hansson begin to sing again, as they always do when they are out in the sleigh.

Just one day, one moment at a time,
O, what comfort whatever us befalls,
For all doth rest in my Father's hands,
Should I, a child, then ever be afraid?

Elizabeth sighs. It is so nice sitting there warm, gliding along in a sleigh while it gets darker and darker in the forest, hearing the singing and the bells tinkling and nothing else.

Soon she falls asleep. She sleeps right up until the sleigh stops at the gate to Primrose Hill.

Inside, in the kitchen, sits Mardie alone with Gossie and Sasso, waiting and waiting. Mummy and Alva and Daddy and lots of other people are out looking for Elizabeth.

It is completely dark, and Mardie is becoming more and more worried. What if they don't find Elizabeth? What if she never comes back, what will happen then?

I guess I'll have to bake her gingerbread too, thinks Mardie. But it doesn't feel as if it would be much fun. Mardie starts to cry. Oh, how she wishes Elizabeth were here!

"Elizabeth, where are you?" she calls, just as if Elizabeth could hear her!

And just then the door opens, and in comes Elizabeth.

"Here I am," she says, laughing.

Then Mardie rushes up and throws her arms around her, and they hug each other long and hard. Finally Elizabeth says:

"I want something to eat!"

"You can have a sandwich!"

Mardie points to the kitchen table, where there is bread and butter and milk and cheese and cold meatballs. And Mardie spreads butter on one slice of bread after the other. Elizabeth cannot get enough. She just eats and eats and she can hardly answer when Mardie asks her:

"But where have you been all day?"

"I've mee niding wian at alled Andersson," says Elizabeth, her mouth full of sandwich. And Mardie understands straightaway what she means.

"I've been riding with a rat called Andersson!"

And while Elizabeth is chewing away, she tells the whole story.

Mardie looks at her reproachfully.

"But you promised Alva that you wouldn't go walking off anywhere!"

"Well, I didn't," says Elizabeth, after thinking carefully for a moment. "I *rode!*"

Then Mardie comes up to her again and gives her another hug.

"You are a horrid child! But I like you anyway."

Mardie lets Elizabeth try her gingerbread, too. Tomorrow she is going to bake her own. But now she is tired and yawning.

"I know what we'll do," says Mardie. "We'll go to bed. And when Mummy and Daddy come home, there'll be two children lying there instead of one. Just think how happy they'll be!"

Elizabeth nods. "Yes, because there's a big difference between two children and just one!"

Now there is no time to lose in getting to bed quickly so that Mummy and Daddy do not get home first and spoil the surprise.

"Can I lie with your arm around me?" asks Elizabeth.

"Yes, of course you can!"

Mardie would like nothing better.

"Because, do you know what? When Mummy and Daddy come home and want to say goodnight to me, they'll see your empty bed and they'll cry."

They giggle with delight at the thought of Mummy and Daddy crying when there is no need at all.

"And then—boff—you stick your head up under my bedclothes and say: 'What are you blubbering about?' They'll split their sides laughing!"

Elizabeth giggles again.

Then she sings the song she has just learned.

Just one day, one moment at a time,
O, what comfort whatever us befalls,
For all doth rest in my Father's hands,
Should I, a child, then ever be afraid?

"Where did you learn that?" asks Mardie. And Elizabeth tells her.

"But Andersson, that rat, he sang one too, he did!"

"Sing it, then," says Mardie.

Elizabeth shakes her head.

"No! It wasn't for children!"

But Mardie persists.

"Bah! Go on, sing it!"

"Under the covers, then, if I'm going to," says Elizabeth.

And they creep under the covers, and Elizabeth sings very, very softly.

Here there's drinking to be done,
Damn it all, it makes life fun…

There she stops abruptly.

"No, it isn't for children. Surely you can hear that!"

"Yes, isn't it awful?" says Mardie. "But sing it once more, anyway."

But Elizabeth won't. She bursts into "Just one day" instead. Then Mardie suddenly remembers something.

"Just think, what if I've given you what I've got and you get sick, too!"

"It won't matter," says Elizabeth. "I'm not going out tomorrow, anyway."

Then she thinks for a moment.

"I'm not going out again before Christmas. And maybe never!"

Mardie is astonished.

"But why?"

"I've been out enough," says Elizabeth.

Mummy and Daddy and Alva come home shortly after. And they're so unhappy that they can't even cry.

Mummy and Daddy go up to the children's room to say goodnight to Mardie.

And in Mardie's bed, they find two small girls lying there close together, asleep. They look almost like angels.

Mummy and Daddy stand there looking at them. They hold each other's hands, and tears trickle down their cheeks.

"Thank heavens," whispers Mummy. "Thank heavens!"

For their certainly *is* a difference between two children and just one.